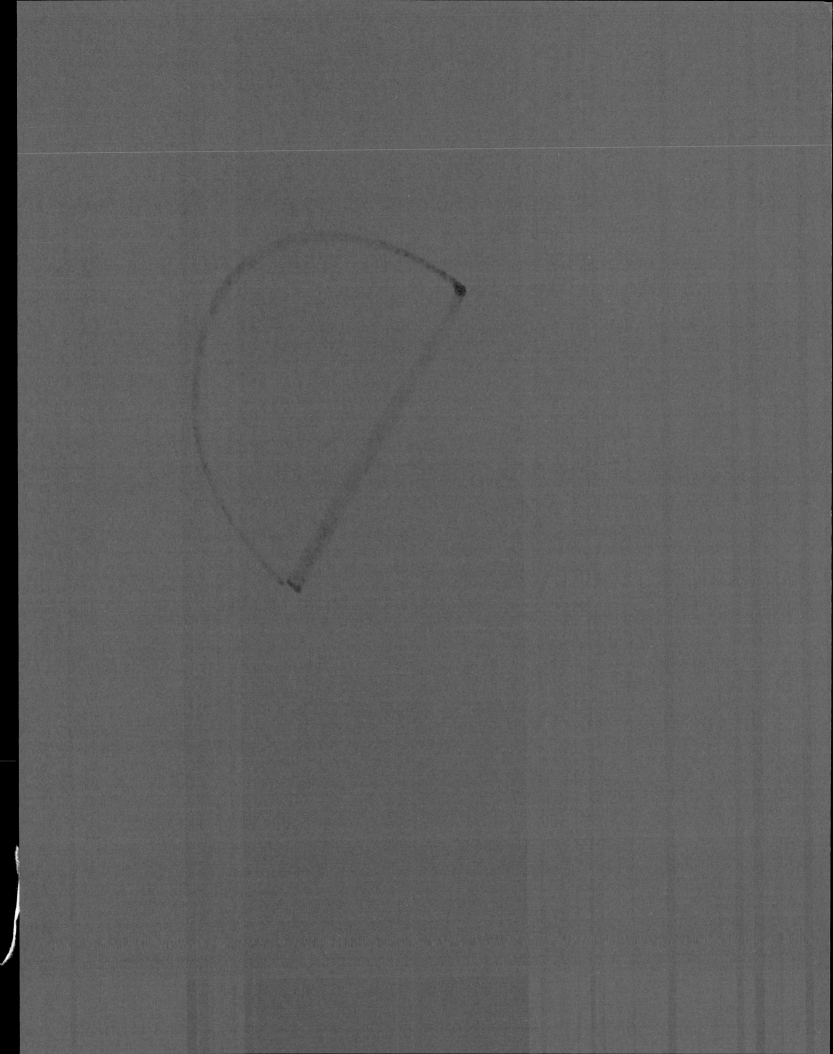

BETH STERN
YODA
GETS A BUDDY

with K. A. Alistir

illustrated by Devin Crane

ALADDIN · New York London Toronto Sydney New Delhi

YUDA was a Persian cat with a very special job:

Watch the claws, Molly!

No biting, Truman!

Kissing, not hissing, Ringo!

He took care of
foster kittens for a nice
lady named Beth.

One morning while Yoda
was taking a quick catnap,
Beth brought a new kitten
to the foster room.

Yoda—who slept with one eye open in case of trouble—
checked him out.
The kitten's name was Buddy.

Ears with soft
fur inside.

Huge smile.

Large, fluffy
paws.

Buddy's smile stretched from whisker to whisker.
Hmm . . . , thought Yoda. Was that a *happy*
smile or a *troublemaker* smile?

Yoda marched over.

"I'm Yoda," he meowed. "I'll be taking care of you while you stay here. I run a tight ship," he continued, "so we'll need to go over some rules."

"Rules are important," agreed Buddy, still smiling.

Hmm . . . , thought Yoda. *The new kitten is smart.*

PAWSITIVELY:
NO BITING!
NO STEALING FOOD!
NO CLIMBING DRAPES!
NO TAIL PULLING!

At lunchtime Buddy waited patiently for his bowl to be filled.

He didn't push or shove, and he cleaned his whiskers when he was done.

Plus, he told the funniest jokes.

What is a cat's
favorite color?
Purrrrple.

What kind of cats go bowling?
Alley cats.

Why did the cat run away
from the tree?
He was afraid of its bark.

Hmm . . . , thought Yoda. *The new kitten is funny.*

At naptime Buddy patted each of the kittens on the head before they dozed off.

They admired Buddy so much, Yoda had an idea.
"Buddy, I love your positive *cattitude*," he said.
"Will you help me watch the other kittens?"

After that, Yoda and Buddy
worked together.
Yoda made sure the kittens
were behaving . . .

while Buddy kept them busy. They followed him
everywhere. Even to the litter box!

Privacy, please!

A few days later Beth brought another new kitten to the foster room.

His name was Frankie.

"What's with his hair?" hissed Truman, pointing.

"I give it two paws down," snorted Ringo.

Sticking-up hair.

Oversized
ears.

Does *not* look like any of the
other foster kittens.

It went from bad to worse. First, the other kittens ate all of Frankie's food. Then they pretended Frankie smelled like stinky cheese and ran away whenever he got too close.

"*Eww!* I think he touched me!" yelped Norman.

"Stay away from Furball Frankie!" shrieked Molly.

What did I ever
do to them?

Frankie hugged his favorite squeaky toy.
Then he slunk off into the corner.

The next day, while Yoda and Buddy were taking their morning nap, the kittens gathered together.

"Let's play a trick on that Furball," whispered Molly. Everyone agreed.

"FRANKIEEEE!" Molly called. "Come play Kitty Ball with us."

As Frankie ran over to the kittens, Ringo raced to the corner and snatched Frankie's squeaky toy!

"Give that back!" Frankie cried.

He chased Ringo to the
top of the kitty condo . . .

under the purple pillow . . .

around the scratching post,
and then . . .

Buddy was drenched!

"We're sorry, Buddy! We were playing a trick on Frankie," explained Molly, "not you."

"Who cares about Frankie, anyway? He's just a funny-looking oddball," said Norman.

Come on, Buddy, smile. What's the big deal?

Yet for a minute the kittens thought soaking-wet Buddy looked a little funny too. It must have been because his fur was wet, right?

But Buddy wasn't happy, and he *wasn't* smiling.

A little while later, after a longer-than-usual grooming session, Buddy finally spoke.

"Do you know why I always pat your heads?" he asked.

"Because you love us!" answered Ringo.

"That's true. But there's another reason," said Buddy, turning to the kittens. "My eyes don't work . . . so I had to figure out another way to see."

Huh?

Was Buddy saying he couldn't see? Did that mean he was blind?

"You're kidding, aren't you?" asked Molly.

But Buddy wasn't kidding.
The kittens were amazed . . . and surprised.
Who would have believed that *Buddy*
was the different one, and wasn't
exactly like them?

Was that what made him—and maybe even
Frankie—so special in the first place?
The kittens sure had plenty to think about.

After that, life in the foster
room wasn't the same. . . .

It was better!

Marching
Mondays:

Bird-watching
Wednesdays:

Frankie Fridays:

One night Yoda and Buddy sat together, watching over the other kittens as they slept.

Buddy really is a remarkable kitten, thought Yoda, smiling. And Buddy smiled back, just as he always had, with his heart.

Dedicated to everyone who comes upon an injured animal and stops to help. —B.S.

I dedicate this book to the love of my life, Whitney Crane. Nothing would be possible without your love and tireless contributions in all that we do! —D.C.

All the author's proceeds from this book will be donated to North Shore Animal League America's Bianca's Furry Friends campaign. To learn more about the campaign, please visit animalleague.org.

THE STORY BEHIND THE STORY

I'll never forget the day one of my Instagram followers asked me for help with a kitten he found in Florida. He sent me a picture of a week-old abandoned kitten, who looked like he had something wrong with his eyes. Howard named him Buddy.

Little Buddy tugged at my heartstrings from the moment I saw him. I knew he needed me. It turned out that his eyes had a severe infection and had to be surgically removed. After the operation, Buddy came to live with us so we could care for and nurture him until he was ready for his forever home.

Fostering is a very emotional experience. I grow very attached to all my foster kittens, but Buddy was *really* special.

While our resident rescue cat, Yoda, was still holding down the fort in the foster room, it was the new foster, Buddy, who was the fun one, teaching the others about unconditional love. All the kittens gravitated to Buddy and emulated everything he did. It was fascinating to watch! As I documented his time with us Buddy captured the admiration and hearts of thousands.

I told Buddy I'd thank everyone who helped him on his journey thus far. Thank you to Carlos, the good and kind man who stopped to help Buddy; thank you to North Shore Animal League America, Joanne, and Cindy; and thank you to Andrea, who transported Buddy and cared for him the few days after his surgery. And to Dr. Jackie Holdsworth, Buddy's veterinarian, who opened her heart and home by adopting this sweet and special kitten after bonding with him during his time in the hospital.

We love you, Buddy! Thank you for encouraging us all to see with our hearts.

ALADDIN An imprint of Simon & Schuster Children's Publishing Division · 1230 Avenue of the Americas, New York, New York 10020
First Aladdin hardcover edition December 2015 · Text copyright © 2015 by BiancaJane, LLC · Illustrations copyright © 2015 by Devin Crane
Back jacket photograph copyright © 2015 by Howard Stern · All rights reserved, including the right of reproduction in whole or in part in any form.
ALADDIN is a trademark of Simon & Schuster, Inc., and related logo is a registered trademark of Simon & Schuster, Inc.
For information about special discounts for bulk purchases, please contact Simon & Schuster Special Sales at 1-866-506-1949 or business@simonandschuster.com.
The Simon & Schuster Speakers Bureau can bring authors to your live event. For more information or to book an event contact
the Simon & Schuster Speakers Bureau at 1-866-248-3049 or visit our website at www.simonspeakers.com.
Designed by Jessica Handelman · The illustrations for this book were rendered digitally. · The text of this book was set in Bembo Infant.
Manufactured in the United States of America 1015 LAK · 2 4 6 8 10 9 7 5 3 1 · Library of Congress Control Number 2015951608
ISBN 978-1-4814-6969-2 (hc) · ISBN 978-1-4814-6970-8 (eBook)